WELL DONE, SECRET SEVEN

ENID BLYTON

*Hodder
Children's
Books*

a division of Hodder Headline Limited

Copyright © Enid Blyton Ltd.

Enid Blyton's signature mark and The Secret Seven are Registered trade
marks of Enid Blyton Ltd.

First published in Great Britain in 1951
by Hodder and Stoughton
This edition 2002

For further information on Enid Blyton, please contact
www.blyton.com

10 9 8 7 6 5 4 3

A Catalogue record for this book is available from the
British Library

ISBN 0 340 79638 3

Typeset by Hewer Text Ltd, Edinburgh
Printed and bound in Great Britain
by Clays Ltd, St Ives plc

The paper and board used in this paperback by Hodder
Children's Books are natural recyclable products made from
wood grown in sustainable forests. The manufacturing processes
conform to the environmental regulations of the country of origin.

Hodder Children's Books
a division of Hodder Headline Limited
338 Euston Road
London NW1 3BH

Contents

[1]

The Secret Seven meet

'Where's my badge? Where's my badge?' said Janet. 'I know I put it into this drawer.' And out of the drawer came handkerchiefs, socks, and ribbons, flying in the air.

'Janet!' said Mummy, crossly. 'Do look what you are doing – I only tidied that drawer this morning. What is it you want – your Secret Seven Badge?'

'Yes! There's a meeting this morning, and I can't go without my badge,' said Janet. 'Peter wouldn't let me into the shed, I know he wouldn't. He's awfully strict about badges.' And away went another shower of handkerchiefs into the air.

'Well, you certainly won't find it in the drawer now,' said Mummy, and she bent and picked up a little round badge with the letters S.S. worked neatly on it. 'You have thrown it out of the drawer with your hankies, silly!'

'Oh, give it to me, Mummy, give it to me!' cried Janet. But Mummy wouldn't.

'No. You pick up all those things first and tidy them in the drawer,' she said.

'But the Secret Seven meet in five minutes!' cried Janet. 'Peter's down in our shed already.'

'Then you can be late,' said Mummy, and walked out of the room with the little badge! Janet groaned. She picked up everything and stuffed it back into the drawer as tidily as she could in a hurry. Then she tore downstairs.

'I've done it, Mummy, and I *promise* I'll do it better when the meeting is over.'

Mummy laughed. She held out the little badge to Janet. 'Here you are. You and your Secret Seven meetings! How you can bear to meet in that stuffy little shed in this hot weather I don't know! *Must* you keep the door *and* the window shut all the time?'

'We have to,' said Janet, pinning on the badge proudly. 'It's a *very* Secret Society, and we can't have anyone listening to our meetings. Not that much has happened lately. We really need something to liven us up – an adventure like the last one.'

'Take the biscuit-tin down with you,' said Mummy. 'And you can have a bottle of orangeade. Here's Scamper come to find you!'

The lovely golden spaniel came trotting into the room. 'Woof,' he said to Janet. 'Woof!'

'Yes, yes – I know I'm late,' said Janet, giving him a pat. 'I suppose Peter sent you to fetch me. Come along. Thanks for the biscuits and orangeade, Mummy.'

She went down the garden path, hugging the biscuit-tin and the bottle of orangeade.

As she came near the shed, she heard voices. It sounded as if all the other six were there!

Janet banged on the door, and Scamper flung himself against it too.

'Password!' yelled six voices.

'Adventure!' yelled back Janet, giving the password for that week. No one could go to a meeting without saying the password.

The door flew open, and Peter, Janet's brother, stood there, frowning. 'Any need to yell out the password like that?' he said.

'Sorry,' said Janet. 'You all yelled out at me, and I just yelled back. Anyway, there's no one to hear. Look, I've brought the biscuit-tin and some orangeade.'

Peter looked to see if she had on her badge. He had seen his sister hunting madly for it ten minutes back, and he had made up his mind he wouldn't allow her in if she hadn't found it. But there it was, pinned to her dress.

Janet went into the shed. Peter shut the

door and bolted it. The window was shut too. The hot summer sun streamed in at the one window, and Janet blew out her cheeks.

'My goodness – it's boiling hot in here! Honestly, I shall melt.'

'We're *all* melting,' said Pam. 'I think this is a silly place to have our weekly meetings when it's so hot. Why can't we have them out in the woods somewhere, in the shade of a tree?'

'No,' said Jack at once. 'My sister Susie would always be hanging around – we wouldn't be a Secret Society any more.'

'Well, couldn't we think of somewhere cool and hidden, where nobody would find us?' said Colin. 'For instance, I've got a hiding-place in my garden where nobody can find me at all, and it's as cool and as hidden as can be.'

'Where is it?' asked Jack.

'Up a tree,' said Colin. 'We've a big tree with some broad branches half-way up, and

I've got a couple of cushions up there, and a box to keep things in. It's cool and breezy, and the branches swing about in the wind. And I've got a really good view all round too. I can always see if anyone is coming!'

They all listened to this speech in silence. Then they looked at one another, their eyes shining.

'Marvellous idea!' Peter said. 'We'll do it ourselves! A house up a tree where we could meet and nobody know! We'll do it!'

[2]

A *wonderful idea*

The Secret Seven discussed the new idea. They all thought it very good indeed. Colin felt very proud to think he had given them such a good idea.

'If we could find a big enough tree, and flat enough branches, we could make a very fine meeting-place there,' said Peter. 'We could take up boards and boxes and cushions, and make a little store-place for biscuits and drinks and books and things.'

'It would be super,' said Janet. 'Nobody would *ever* guess we were there, and nobody could possibly hear what we say.'

'Let's get out of this hot shed and go and find somewhere now,' said Colin. 'I know exactly what an ice-cream feels like when it begins to melt. As for poor old Scamper, he's panting as if he's run a race.'

So he was. His pink tongue hung out, long and wavy, and he panted loudly. Peter got up.

'Come on, old boy. You can have a drink at the stream when we go past.'

They took the biscuit-tin with them, but they all had a drink of the orangeade before they left. Scamper rushed on to the stream as soon as he knew they were going that way.

'Hey! – don't drink *all* the stream!' called Peter. Scamper lapped and lapped. They went on their way and left him still lapping.

'We'll go to Windy Woods,' said Colin. 'There are some enormous trees there, easy to climb too.'

They came to Windy Woods. It was cool and shady there. 'Now let's look carefully and see if we can spot a good tree,' said Jack. 'Big enough to hold all the Secret Seven!'

'What about Scamper?' said Janet, suddenly. 'He can't climb a tree. He won't be able to come to the meetings.'

'We could make him a sort of harness, and pull him up,' said George.

'He'd hate that,' said Peter. 'Anyway he's not really a member. He needn't come. Or he could sit at the bottom of the tree and guard us.'

'Oh yes! He could bark if anyone came near,' said Barbara. 'He would be a fine gate-keeper.'

'Tree-keeper!' said Pam. 'Look, what about *this* tree? It's enormous.'

'No good,' said Peter, looking up at the great beech. 'No low-down branches to climb up on. We must have a tree that's easy to climb, or we'll spend all our time getting up and down.'

They separated, and began to look for likely trees. There didn't seem to be so many after all. George found one that he thought was just right, but when he climbed up a little way he soon saw that it was impossible to have any kind of house up there.

'No good!' he called down. 'The branches criss-cross too much and are far too thick.'

Down he came, and then Jack shouted out. 'Come here, all of you. What about *this* tree?'

They ran up and looked at Jack's tree. 'Yes,' said Colin, 'that really does look a likely one. One low branch waist-high to climb on – places to put your feet up the trunk after that – another branch there to cling to – and what looks like a nice lot of flattish branches half-way up. I'll shin up and see.'

'No, I'll go,' said Jack. 'I found it. You come after.'

He stood on the low branch and then made his way up, putting his feet on to jutting-out pieces of the trunk that really seemed made for footholds! Boughs spread out in just the right places to hold on to, and then Jack came to the place where branches grew out level from the great tree trunk.

'It's fine!' he called down. 'There are about six branches here, all on the same level, more or less, and there's a hole in the trunk too. It would make a fine cupboard. Come on up! There's room for everyone!'

The others climbed up in excitement. Peter came last of all, in case anyone got stuck and wanted help. But it was such an easy tree to climb that nobody wanted any help at all.

'It's the biggest tree in the wood, I should think,' said Peter, when they were all sitting on the platform of branches. 'What luck to have so many broad branches all about the same level. Where's the hole you told us about, Jack?'

'Here,' said Jack, and moved away from the part of the trunk he was leaning against.

The others saw a very large hole. Jack thrust his hand in and felt round it.

'It goes down about a metre – or just under,' he said. 'It would make a good store-place for us, just what we want. Well, shall we make this our Secret Seven Tree, our new meeting-place?'

'Oh *yes*,' said everyone at once, and they began to talk about what they would do to make it a proper tree-house.

Peter took out a notebook. 'Now,' he said, 'suggestions and ideas one at a time please. I'll write them all down.'

[3]

The big tree

Everyone was full of ideas. 'We could bring some small boards to put across the branches and make a proper little platform,' said Colin. 'We've got some in our shed at home.'

'And rope to tie them on with,' said Jack.

'Yes, and cushions to sit on,' said Pam. 'Only we'd have to stuff them in the hole in the tree whenever we left, in case it rained.'

'Can't do that. The hole's not big enough,' said Jack.

'Well, I could bring an old waterproof sheet – a rubber one – to cover up any of our things when we leave,' said Barbara. 'Then they would be quite all right.'

'Good idea,' said Peter, scribbling fast in his notebook. 'Any more ideas?'

'Stores for the cubby-hole in the tree,' said Janet. 'Unbreakable mugs and things like that. I'll bring those. Mummy always lets us have them when we want them, so long as we take them back sometime.'

'This is fine,' said Peter, scribbling quickly. 'Boards to make a platform. You can bring those, Colin.'

'Rope to tie them with,' said Jack. 'I'll bring that.'

'Cushions for me,' said Pam.

'Rubber sheet for me,' said Barbara.

'Mugs for me,' said Janet. 'What about you, George?'

'I'll bring some food for the cubby-hole,' said George.

'Great!' said Peter. 'And I'll bring the drinks. Gosh, we're going to have a glorious time. It will be a wonderful meeting-place.

Don't you go and tell that awful sister of yours, Jack.'

'As if I'd tell Susie!' said Jack, indignantly. 'When shall we begin to make the tree-house?'

'Why not tomorrow?' said Peter. 'Nobody is going away on holiday just yet. It shouldn't take us long to put everything together up here. This place is just *made* for a tree-house!'

A loud and mournful howl rose up from the foot of the tree. Then there came a scrabbling noise.

'Oh, poor Scamper!' said Janet. 'He's been as good as anything waiting for us. I guess he wishes he could climb like our cat. He'd be up beside us in half a jiffy!'

'We're coming, Scamper,' called Peter. He took one last look round the tree. 'It really couldn't be better,' he said. 'And there's only one more thing to hope for.'

'What's that?' asked Jack, beginning to climb down.

'Something for the Secret Seven to *do*,' said Peter. 'We haven't had any adventure or mystery or excitement for ages.'

'I'm glad you said that,' said Pam. 'When you say things never happen – they always do!'

'I hope you're right,' said Peter. He parted the leaves of the tree behind him. 'What a long way we can see!' he said. 'Right over the wood, and across to the hill. I can see the road winding up the hill too, and cars on it.'

'Come on,' called Jack, who was half-way down the tree now. 'It's getting late. I shall get into a row, I know I shall. My mother says our meetings always last an hour too long!'

'Well, this was a really good one any-how,' said Colin, slithering down much too fast. 'Gosh, now I've torn my shorts.'

'I should think so, going down the tree as if it was a slippery-slip!' said Barbara.

Scamper gave them a tremendous welcome. He leapt on one after another as the Secret Seven jumped down to the ground, barking and licking with all his might. Peter laughed.

'Poor old Scamper – you won't like our new meeting-place, will you? Hey – look – what about giving Scamper that hole over there as a kind of kennel when we are up the tree?'

He pointed to what looked almost like a small cave in a nearby tree. It was old and rotten, and a hole had appeared at the foot of its trunk. It would just about fit Scamper.

'We could put one of his rugs in there, and a bone, so that he would know it was his place,' said Peter. 'And we could say, "On guard, Scamper!" to him, so that he would stay there till we came down.'

'Oh *yes* – he would be our sentinel,' said

George. 'He'd make an awfully good one. He would bark as soon as anyone came near.'

They all felt happy now that they had made a good plan for Scamper. He wouldn't be able to come up the tree and join their meetings as he did in the shed – but at least he would be doing *something* for them and feeling important because he was on guard.

'Woof,' said Scamper, exactly as if he understood every word, and agreed thoroughly. He wagged his tail and ran in front of them. *He* knew it was dinner-time, if they didn't!

[4]

Making the tree-house

The next day was really very exciting. If anyone had been in Windy Woods he or she would have been most astonished to see the file of children going down the path, each carrying some kind of load.

They had all met at Peter's house with their goods. Janet, his sister, had mugs and plates and spoons. Colin had a set of boards, which Jack had to help him with. Jack had coiled yards and yards of rope round his waist and looked really most peculiar.

Barbara was carrying a big rubber sheet carefully folded, and she was helping Pam with a set of old cushions.

'They're a bit dirty and flattened out,'

said Pam, 'but I didn't think that would matter. I got them out of the garden shed, they've been there ages. I could only find six, so we'll have to get another somewhere.'

Janet ran to get one from her garden shed, where the Secret Seven usually held their meetings. That made seven cushions, one for everyone.

George had some chocolate, and also a great big tin of mixed biscuits. 'Mother gave me them,' he said. 'She says your mother keeps supplying our Society with food, and it's her turn now.'

'Wonderful,' said Peter, with much approval. 'What a smashing tin!' He had taken some money from his money-box and bought a bottle of lemonade and one of orangeade, and he also had two bottles full of water to use with the drinks.

Even Scamper had to carry something! He had one of his little rugs rolled up tightly and tied with string. He was carrying it in his mouth, feeling most important. He loved it when the children really let him take part in everything they were doing.

'Woooooof-woof,' he said, with his mouth full of rug.

'He says he likes to be carrying something like everyone else,' said Janet. 'That's right, isn't it, Scamper?'

Scamper wagged his tail, and almost dropped his rug in his longing to bark properly. 'Ooooof,' he said.

The Seven set off down the path, came to Windy Woods, and made their way to their tree.

'We ought to carve S.S. on the trunk, for Secret Seven,' said Pam.

'Well, we can't,' said Peter. 'My father says that scribbling on walls and pavements and carving on trees is only done by idiots. And if anyone in the Secret Seven wants to be an idiot he can jolly well get out.'

'I only said we *ought* to carve S.S.,' said
Pam, quite hurt. 'I didn't mean that we
should. You know I'm not a hooligan.'

'Yes. I do know,' said Peter. 'I was only
just telling you what my father said. Let's
make Scamper his little sentry-box place
before we go up the tree.'

It was fun showing Scamper his 'sentry-
box'. He sniffed all round, and then sat
down at the entrance, his mouth open as
if he were smiling.

'He's pleased. He's smiling,' said Janet.
'Come out, Scamper and we'll put your rug
in. Then you'll know this is your own place
– your sentry-box. And you're the sentinel
on guard. ON GUARD, Scamper. You know
what that means, don't you?'

'Woof,' said Scamper, and looked suddenly serious. He ran out.

Peter stuffed his rug into the hole. Then
he dropped a bone there for Scamper, and
then he put an old cap of his in the hole too.

'On guard, Scamper,' he said, pointing. 'On guard, old fellow. Very important. Guard my cap for me till I come back. On guard!'

Scamper went back into the hole, sniffed solemnly at the cap, then at the bone. He turned round and sat himself upright at the entrance to the hole again, looking important. Nothing would now make him leave his 'sentry-box' until Peter told him he might. He was a very, very good guard when he knew he had to be.

'Now we can get on with our own job without old Scamper leaping round us and barking and getting in the way all the time,' said Peter. 'Let's tie the boards and the rubber sheet to the ropes – then one of us can go up the tree with the rope-end, and pull the whole lot up at once.'

This seemed a very good idea, but wasn't. Peter didn't tie the ropes securely enough round the boards – and as Jack was hauling the package up the tree, a rope slipped and down came all the boards and the rubber sheet, bumping and slipping against the tree!

One board hit Colin on the shoulder, and the rubber sheet unfolded and fell neatly over Pam's head. The others squealed with laughter as Pam yelled and struck out, wondering what had happened to her.

'Oh dear – sorry!' said Peter, pulling the sheet off poor Pam. 'We'll tie the things more firmly this time.'

'You let *me* tie them,' said Colin, rubbing his shoulder. 'I'm not going to have a shower of heavy boards fall on me again!'

'This is *fun*,' said George. 'This is really *fun*! I bet nobody ever had such fun making a tree-house before!'

[5]

Great fun

All the Seven really enjoyed themselves making the tree-house. It took them the whole of the morning. Placing the boards and roping them firmly in place wasn't quite so easy as they had thought it would be.

The boards kept slipping about, and had a most annoying habit of falling down the tree and having to be fetched up again. Every time one fell, Scamper barked to tell them.

'He probably thinks we don't notice when a board falls down,' said Janet, with a giggle. 'Oh dear – whose turn is it to climb down after that one?'

'It seems to me that it's a question of too

many cooks spoiling the broth,' said Jack. 'With all of us sitting about on the branches that we want to put the boards on it's really difficult. You girls get down to lower branches. Go on. Four of us up here are enough to rope down the boards.'

The girls climbed down a little, putting themselves the other side of the tree for safety. 'Bother! There goes one of the cushions!' said Pam. 'Well, it can wait. There'll be another board falling down in a minute, and whoever gets that can get the cushion too.'

The boys had a fine old time putting the boards in place, and roping them firmly to make a kind of platform. At last they had done the job really well.

'Quite safe now,' said Jack, testing the platform by walking over it slowly. 'Nobody is going to slip down between two boards, and no board is going to get out of place. We've done a really good job.'

The girls came up and admired the platform. The cushion was rescued from the ground below, and soon the wooden platform looked quite cosy, set out with seven rather dirty, flat cushions.

The mugs, plates, drinks, biscuit-tin and packets of chocolate were put into the convenient cubby-hole. The rubber sheet was neatly tied to a branch ready to be spread over the cushions and platform when the Seven left.

'There!' said Peter, pleased. 'Our new headquarters, Meeting-Place of the Secret Seven Society. Sentinel on guard down below. Everything ready to tackle our next adventure, if only it comes!'

'I don't mind if it doesn't,' said Pam. 'This is enough adventure for me. Fancy having a tree-house like this! Ah – here comes the wind!'

A gust blew strongly, and the branches of the big tree rocked and shook. The platform rocked too.

'Lovely!' said Janet, as she felt the platform moving. 'I feel as if I'm on a ship now – that swaying feeling is just like being in a boat.'

'It's half-past twelve,' said Peter. 'Let's have a biscuit and a drink, and go home. We can come back this afternoon. We'll bring books and a game and enjoy ourselves.'

'It's funny how grown-ups don't like us to eat just before we have a meal, in case we can't eat our dinner or tea afterwards,' said Janet, nibbling a biscuit. 'I could eat six of these super biscuits and still feel hungry for my lunch.'

'Well, one is all you're going to have,' said Peter, putting the lid on hastily. 'If we eat six at a time there soon won't be any left. A big tin like this ought to last us for ages!'

In the afternoon they all went back to the tree-house. Scamper took his place down below as sentinel again. He seemed quite to understand, and wagged his tail cheerily as one by one the Secret Seven went up the tree.

The wind was stronger in the afternoon, and it was very pleasant to feel the platform rocking. 'I almost expect to hear a splash of water,' said Janet. 'It's so like a boat. I love it!'

They sat or lay about on the platform on their cushions, reading or talking, nibbling at some of George's chocolate. It was nice to hear the wind rustling the leaves round them, and to feel the breeze in their hair.

And then suddenly Scamper began barking down below. 'Wuff-wuff, woof, woof, WOOF! Wuff-wuff-woof-woof-WOOF!'

'What's up with Scamper?' said Peter, and he peered cautiously down the tree. He heard a voice.

'Now then – what's up with *you*! Don't you come near me or my kitten!'

'It's a boy,' whispered Peter to the others.

'A scruffy-looking boy. He's got a kitten cuddled into his neck. Scamper's leaping round him like anything.'

'He won't hurt him,' whispered back George. 'I expect he's stopping him climbing this tree! He may have thought the boy wanted to. Where's the kitten? Move over and let me see.'

Peter wouldn't move over, so George gave him a shove. Peter clutched at one of the ropes that held a board, and his board tipped up. He almost shot headlong down the tree, but just stopped himself in time by clutching at a branch.

Pam squealed in fright. Peter gave her a sharp nudge. 'Quiet!' he hissed. 'Do you want our hiding-place discovered on the very first day?'

The boy on the ground below looked round, startled by Pam's squeal. He couldn't think where it had come from. Then he looked up the tree.

'Hey!' he called. 'Anyone up there? Who is it?'

Nobody said a word. Pam held her breath until she thought she would burst. Peter glared at her.

'Is anyone up there?' shouted the boy. 'I'm coming up to see.'

Peter gave a low groan. Just what he had been afraid of!

But Scamper had other ideas. What! Let a strange boy climb up the tree he was guarding! What nonsense!

Scamper leapt at the boy, growling. He didn't mean to bite him or even to snap – but the boy didn't know that. He had just put up an arm to get hold of the lowest branch of the tree. He put it down in a hurry and faced Scamper.

'What's the matter? What are you so excited about? Get down. If you're after my kitten you can think again. Get down I say!'

But not until the boy had walked right away from the tree did Scamper stop leaping and barking. As soon as he saw that the stranger no longer meant to climb, Scamper became his own friendly self again. He placed himself between the tree and the boy and wagged his tail.

'I don't know why you won't let me climb that tree, but if you don't want me to, I won't,' the Seven heard the boy say. 'I can always come back when you're not here if I want to, anyway! I'm going now. You've frightened my poor little kitten nearly to death!'

The Seven heard the crackling of twigs and pine-needles as the boy walked away. Scamper gave one bark of warning, and then went back to his 'sentry-box', very pleased with himself indeed. Aha! He was a fine sentinel. No one could climb that tree unless he let them.

The Seven said nothing until there was no

further sound from down below. Pam spoke first. She looked as if she was going to cry.

'I'm sorry, I'm sorry! Don't tell me off! I thought you were going to fall down the tree, Peter, and I couldn't HELP squealing.'

'Well, next time you squeal you'll be turned out of the Secret Society,' said Peter. 'Giving away our marvellous tree-house the very first day we make it!'

Pam went very red. 'I promise I won't do it again,' she said, in a small voice. 'Anyway, the boy's gone, so no harm's done.'

'Thanks to Scamper,' said Peter, still annoyed. 'And how do you know the boy won't come back when we're gone?'

'He won't remember the tree,' said Pam. 'Don't make such a fuss, Peter. I feel bad enough about it anyway.'

'Have some more chocolate,' said George, anxious to change the subject. He didn't want anyone to remind him that it was because of his violent shove Peter had nearly fallen down the tree, and so made Pam squeal.

'Thanks,' said Peter, and took some chocolate. So did everyone, and immediately felt better. They nibbled and talked about how marvellous Scamper was as a guard.

'I bet he's gone back to his sentry-box and is sitting up there as alert as can be,' said Jack. 'I wish I had a dog like him. He's wonderful.'

'*I* don't think that boy will come back,' said Colin after a time. 'I think he was probably just having a walk through the woods – with his kitten! Funny thing to take a kitten about when you go for a walk.'

'Let's have a game of cards,' said Pam. 'I've brought some. And what about a drink? I'm awfully thirsty.'

It really was fun up in the tree-house. They drank orangeade, crunched up a chocolate biscuit each and played a rather tiresome game of cards. The wind would keep flipping the cards off the platform and blowing them down the tree.

'I feel that dominoes would be better,' said George at last. 'At least they wouldn't blow off so easily. Bother – there goes one of my cards again. I'll bring some dominoes tomorrow.'

At five o'clock it was time to go home. They put the cushions in a neat pile and tied the rubber sheet over them. They put everything else away into the tree-hole. A small grey squirrel suddenly ran up a bough and looked at them in amazement.

'Hello!' said Peter. 'How are you? And how's your family? Don't you dare rob our cubby-hole!'

The squirrel chattered a little, and then disappeared with a beautiful bound. Everyone laughed, and Scamper heard them from his post down below. He barked.

'All right, Scamper! We're coming!' called Peter. 'And we'll bring you a chocolate biscuit for being such a good guard. Here we come!'

[6]

Next morning

The next morning they all met at Peter's house again and went off to Windy Woods. Some of them had things to eat, and Peter had the drinks again. Janet had a big book with her. She had promised to lend it to Colin for the day.

'Here's Daddy's book that I told you about,' she said. 'It's all about ships – every single ship there is. I told you I'd bring it to show you. But Daddy says I've GOT to give it back to him in two or three days' time. So don't keep it too long.'

'Thanks awfully,' said Colin, and took it, very pleased. He loved ships, and this was really a wonderful book. He knew he must be very careful with it indeed.

Scamper trotted with them, as usual. They came to Windy Woods and made their way to their tree. Scamper at once put himself into his 'sentry-box' and sat there, serious and important.

'Woof,' he said, and Janet patted him.

'Yes, we know you'll be on guard,' she said. 'Good dog!'

They all climbed up. Peter undid the rubber sheet from the cushions and spread them out over the platform. Just as he had finished the girls gave a startled cry. 'Look! The lid of the biscuit-tin is off, and most of the biscuits are gone! We left quite a lot, but only a few are here. And some of the chocolate we left is gone too, and the lemonade bottle is empty. It was half-full.'

They all looked into the cubby-hole. Yes – the biscuits were certainly gone. The Secret Seven looked at one another. Then Janet spoke suddenly.

'Do you know what I think? I think it's

that cheeky little squirrel! I bet he came here after we had gone, looked into our cubby-hole, and took our things. Squirrels are very clever!'

'But what about the lemonade?' asked Peter, doubtfully.

'Squirrels use their paws like monkeys,' said Janet. 'We've seen them holding nuts in their paws and chewing them. I'm sure that squirrel would be clever enough to take the cork out of the bottle. I expect it emptied some of the lemonade out. It wouldn't like the taste.'

'I can believe in a squirrel that takes a cork out of a bottle and even empties some of the lemonade out,' said Peter. 'But I can't somehow believe in a squirrel that puts the cork back again. I believe it's that boy!'

'So do I,' said George. But the others didn't. They were sure it was the squirrel.

'Anyway, don't let's worry,' said Jack. 'We've got plenty of food today. If the squirrel likes a few biscuits and a bit of chocolate, he can have them.'

They had been sensible that morning and had brought dominoes to play with. However, they could just as well have brought cards, because there was no wind. The sun was not to be seen, and the clouds were low.

'I hope it's not going to rain,' said Colin, looking up. 'I believe it is.'

'Well, we shan't feel it much, hidden away in the middle of a thick old tree,' said Pam. 'I don't expect we'll get a single drop on our platform.'

When it did begin to rain, and the drops pattered on the leaves, only one or two got through to their platform. But Colin was worried.

'I'd better put this ship book into the cubby-hole,' he said. 'Hadn't I, Janet? Your father might be cross if it got wet.'

'Well he would,' said Janet. 'He's very

careful about books. Put it at the back of the cubby-hole, then it won't even get a drop.'

So the game was stopped while Colin tucked the big book away very carefully behind the little pile of food in the hole. The rain came down harder. It was rather fun to sit and listen to it pelting down on the leaves, and yet get hardly a drop on the platform.

By dinner-time the rain had stopped. 'We'd better make a dash for it now,' said Peter, trying to peer through the branches to see if there was any blue sky. 'Now what about our things? Do you suppose it's safe to leave them, after some of the biscuits and chocolates have been taken?'

'Quite safe,' said Pam, horrified at the thought of dragging everything down the tree to take home. 'If the squirrel – or whoever the thief was – didn't take the cushions or the mugs and things yesterday it's not likely he will today. And we've only left a few biscuits.'

'Right,' said Peter. 'We'll just tie up the cushions in the rubber sheet and go. Scamper! We're coming!'

'Woof!' said Scamper, and they heard him leaping up at the tree-trunk. He had been very bored in his sentry-box all by himself.

They went down the tree carefully, because the rain had made parts of it rather slippery. Scamper gave them a most hilarious welcome.

They all went off to their homes, and alas, nobody noticed that Colin wasn't carrying the book of ships. He had forgotten all about it, and it was still tucked away in the cubby-hole half-way up the great big tree.

[7]

Windy Woods at night

It wasn't until Colin was undressing for bed that night that he suddenly remembered the book of ships. Where was it?

Then, with a shock, he knew. He had left it in the tree-house cubby-hole. How dreadful! Suppose that mischievous squirrel found it and tore the pages or nibbled at them! Suppose a storm came and blew rain into the hole and spoilt the book! How angry Janet's father would be!

Colin dressed hurriedly again. He must go and get the book. But he had reckoned without his family. They seemed to be continually moving about the house that night, running upstairs, standing in the hall, going in and out of the garden. It was maddening.

Colin sat by his window till half-past ten. Would his tiresome family never, never go to bed? Ah, that sounded like Granny coming upstairs.

It wasn't until eleven o'clock that Colin felt it was safe to slip out of the house. He got safely out into the garden and jumped when an owl hooted suddenly. He stopped.

Would he know the way to the tree in the dark? It was almost dark now, and in the wood it would be pitch-black. Colin felt a nasty little stab of fear. It wouldn't really be very nice in Windy Woods at night. Suppose he missed the way, didn't find the tree, and got lost? He really would feel an awful idiot, and his mother would be worried and cross.

He had to pass Peter's farm on the way. He wondered if Peter was awake. If he was, he would go with him, he was sure. He stepped into Peter's garden and made his way quietly to the farmhouse. He knew where Peter's bedroom was.

The farmhouse was in complete darkness. Everyone was in bed. Colin took up a few small pebbles and threw one carefully at Peter's window. It fell back again. Colin threw another, waiting for it to hit the window.

But it didn't. The window was open and the pebble flew inside and hit Peter neatly on the cheek, as he slept peacefully in bed.

He woke with a jump, sat up and stared crossly round the dark room. He rubbed his cheek, wondering what had happened. Another pebble came in at the window and hit the wall.

'Hallo! Someone's throwing stones!' said Peter to himself, and he went cautiously to the window. He made out someone standing below.

'Who is it?' whispered Peter as loudly as he could without making too much noise.

'It's me, Colin!' came a whisper from below. 'Peter, listen – I've left your father's book in the tree-house, in the cubby-hole. I must get it. Will you come with me?'

'Oooh yes,' said Peter, thrilled at the idea of going into Windy Woods at night and climbing up into the tree-house. It would be quite an adventure! Lovely!

He slipped on a jumper and a pair of jeans, and shinned down the tree that grew obligingly outside his window. In a moment he and Colin were slipping down the path like shadows.

Colin felt perfectly brave the moment that Peter was with him. 'I was afraid I might not find the tree,' he whispered, as they padded along. 'You're so good at finding your way, and I thought you'd know it even in the dark.'

'Yes, I shall,' said Peter. 'But anyway I've brought a torch with me. This is fun, isn't it?'

They came to Windy Woods, which were

quiet tonight. Very little wind was about, and the trees made hardly any noise. An owl hooted again and made both boys jump. 'I'm glad I'm not a mouse,' said Peter. 'I should be scared stiff of an owl's hoot!'

They came to their tree. Peter went up first, shining the torch down now and again for Colin, who found it difficult to climb in the dark. At last they came to the platform. It looked strange and desolate in the light of Peter's torch.

'Now to get the book,' said Colin, and he shone the torch in at the hole. He gave a sudden exclamation.

'Hey! Someone's been here again! Everything is upside down and muddled up as if someone's been hunting for something. Food probably.'

'Well, we didn't leave much,' said Peter. 'Bother! It can't be that squirrel. It must be someone who has discovered our tree-house. Is your book there?'

'Yes, thank goodness,' said Colin. 'Peter, *who* comes here? It's maddening!'

'Can't think,' said Peter. And then he heard a sound that astonished him. It was a very small sound indeed, and it came from somewhere in the tree.

'Did you hear that?' whispered Peter. 'It sounded like a tiny mew, but there can't be a cat up here!'

He swung his torch round and about to see if he could find a hidden cat, and then he suddenly clutched Colin and pointed silently.

In the light of his torch was a pair of bare feet! Someone – *someone*, was sitting silently on a branch above them, his feet showing in the torchlight. Who *could* he be?

[8]

Someone in the tree-house

Peter suddenly made a grab for the two bare feet and caught hold of them. There was a yell, and the feet began to kick out. But Peter held them tightly.

'You come on down,' he said, angrily. 'Who are you? How dare you come to our tree-house and mess our things up. Come on down!'

'Let me go,' said a boy's voice, and then there came a mewing noise again, and to the two boys' surprise a small kitten leapt down to a nearby branch and stared at Peter and Colin with wide-open green eyes.

'A kitten!' said Colin. 'It must be that boy with the kitten! He did come back after all!'

'Don't pull me, don't pull me!' called the boy on the bough above. 'I'm slipping.'

Peter let go his feet. 'Come on down then, and don't play the fool, because we're two to one,' he said.

The feet came down lower, then the legs, and then a thin body. Then came the whole boy, looking scared and white-faced.

'Sit down,' ordered Peter. 'Don't move. Now you just tell us what you're doing in our tree.'

The boy sat down. He looked up at them sulkily. He was thin and pale, and his hair wanted cutting.

'I only came here to hide,' he said. 'I've not done any harm, except to take a few biscuits last night. But if you'd been as hungry as I was, you'd have taken them too.'

'What are you hiding from?' asked Colin. 'Have you run away from home or something?'

'I shan't tell you anything,' said the boy. 'You might tell the police.'

'We shan't,' said Colin. 'At least, not if we can help it. Why should we tell the police anyhow?'

The kitten crept quietly back to the boy and cuddled into his coat. Colin and Peter saw that it had a bleeding leg. The boy put up his hand and stroked it gently. It began to purr.

Both Colin and Peter suddenly felt certain that the boy couldn't be terribly bad because he so obviously loved the kitten – and the kitten trusted him. They stared at the sullen boy.

'Go on – tell us,' said Peter, keeping the light of his torch full on the boy. 'We might be able to help you.'

'Will you let me stay here at night?' asked the boy. 'In case they find me. They know I'm somewhere in Windy Woods.'

'Who?' asked Peter. 'Tell us everything. What's your name, to begin with?'

'Jeff,' said the boy, still stroking the kitten. 'It all began when my mother went to hospital. I lived with her. My dad's dead, so there's only us two. But when Mum was taken to hospital I was sent to my Uncle Harry and my Aunt Lizzy.'

'Well, go on,' said Peter. 'Why did you run away?'

'I stayed there a week,' said Jeff, 'and my mother didn't come out of hospital, and nobody would tell me anything. Suppose she never came out? What was I to do? All I had was my kitten.'

'Well, wouldn't your uncle and aunt have looked after you?' asked Peter.

'I didn't want them to,' said Jeff. 'They are bad. My mother always said so, and she knew. They've got bad friends, and they do bad things.'

'What do they do?' asked Peter.

'Oh – steal – and worse things,' said Jeff. 'They were all right to me, I mean they gave me food, and my aunt mended some of my clothes, but they were cruel to my kitten.'

Colin and Peter stared at Jeff in sympathy. Peter knew how he would have felt if someone had been unkind to Scamper. 'Did – did they hurt the kitten's leg where it's bleeding?' he asked.

Jeff nodded. 'Yes. Uncle kicked at it. It's not so bad now, but it was very bad at first. So that day I ran away, and took the kitten with me. I hid in an empty house, first, but they came after me. Then I came to this wood, and guessed you were up this tree, when your dog barked. So when you'd gone I climbed up.'

'I see,' said Peter. 'And ate our biscuits and chocolate. But why are your uncle and aunt bothering about you? They know you can go back when you want to.'

''Tisn't my aunt,' said Jeff. 'It's my uncle

and his friend Mr Tizer. They're afraid I know too much.'

'Too much about what?' asked Colin.

'I used to sleep in the sitting-room,' explained Jeff. 'And one night I heard them talking about some plan they were making. I just heard a few things – but I couldn't make head or tail of them. I turned over to get more comfortable, and my uncle jumped up and accused me of listening.'

'Ah, and now that you've run away they're afraid you will tell someone what you heard,' said Colin. 'Did you hear much?'

'No – nothing to make any sense,' said Jeff. 'But they don't believe that, and they're after me. I saw Mr Tizer in the woods today with his dog. They're hunting me, and I'm scared. That's why I came up to your tree-house. Can't I stay?'

'Yes – you stay here for the night,' said Peter. 'Get out the cushions. Make yourself comfortable. And tomorrow we'll all come and think what to do! Don't you worry – the Secret Seven will put things right!'

[9]

Another meeting

Peter and Colin helped the boy to get out the cushions from the rubber sheet. The kitten sat on a nearby branch, watching. It was a dear little thing, a fluffy tabby.

'You can have the rest of our biscuits, and a drink too, if you want to,' said Colin. 'Oh! – I nearly forgot that ship book! I *must* get it out of the cubby-hole!'

He pulled it out, and then the two boys began to climb down the tree again, feeling carefully for foot-holds. It wasn't nearly so easy to climb down in the dark as it was in the daylight!

'Good night,' called the boy, gratefully. 'And thanks for your help. Are you coming tomorrow? Could you bring me a spot of milk for my kitten, please?'

'Yes, of course – and a bit of fish if we can,' called back Peter. 'Don't fall out of the tree when you're asleep.'

'No, I shan't,' said the boy, sounding much more cheerful.

Colin and Peter made their way home, talking in low voices about the boy and his curious story.

'What do you suppose his uncle and that friend of his – Mr Tizer – were planning to do, and were afraid Jeff had overheard?' said Peter. 'If it was a robbery or something we ought to try and stop it.'

'Well – if we *can* find out anything from Jeff, I really do think we ought to tell someone,' said Colin. 'Your parents, for instance.'

'Yes. But it would be nice to see if the Secret Seven can do something about it first,' said Peter. 'We'll call a meeting tomorrow – up the tree, with Jeff there – and we'll see what we can get out of him. He must have heard *something* that was said!'

'Right,' said Colin, beginning to feel excited. 'This is great! Just when we thought nothing would ever happen, something does. Do you want me to go and tell everyone tomorrow morning that something is up, and we must meet at the tree?'

'Yes,' said Peter. 'Passwords and everything. I'll be at the bottom of the tree, and nobody must yell out the password – just whisper it. Badges must be worn too.'

'Good,' said Colin, pleased. 'Well, we'll say good night here – this is your gate, isn't it? Good thing I went back for this book tonight, wasn't it? We wouldn't have caught Jeff if I hadn't.'

The boys went their different ways, and Peter wondered whether or not to wake Janet and tell her about the boy in the tree-house, but he decided not to. It would keep till morning.

All the Secret Seven were excited next morning when they heard about the meeting to be held, and were told about Jeff.

'Can we take Scamper with us, do you think?' asked Pam. 'Do you suppose he would frighten the kitten?'

'No. He's nice with kittens,' said Peter. 'Anyway, he'll be on guard down below, and the kitten will be up the tree with Jeff. I must remember to take a bottle of milk, and a saucer, and some fish.'

'Good thing we had haddock for breakfast,' said Janet. 'I'll wrap a bit up in greaseproof paper. Poor little kitten! Do you suppose its leg will be all right? Imagine anyone kicking a *kitten*!'

Promptly at ten o'clock the Secret Seven met at the foot of the tree. The password was whispered importantly to Peter.

'Adventure!'

'Adventure!'

'Adventure! Is that boy up there?'

'Yes. Got your badge on? Good. Are we all here now? Well, up we go. Scamper, on guard, please!'

Scamper looked at Peter, wagged his tail, and at once ran to his sentry-box in the nearby tree. He sat down on his bit of rug there, and looked quite stern as if to say, 'Strangers, beware! I'm on guard. Grrrrrrrrr!'

Peter went up the tree first, the bottle of milk in his pocket, and the little saucer between his teeth. The others followed. Peter saw Jeff peering down anxiously as he heard them climbing up.

'Hello, Jeff!' said Peter, clambering up on to the platform of boards. 'Had a good night? How's the kitten?'

'Its leg is much better,' said Jeff. 'And I slept all night except when the wind blew too hard. I say – nobody will give me away will they? How many of you are there?'

'Seven,' said Peter. 'Move up a bit, Jeff,

and make room. We're a Secret Society – the Secret Seven. We have our password and badges, and we hold meetings. If anything turns up for us to do, we do it.'

Jeff sat at the back of the platform and looked at each member climbing up. Colin he knew from the night before. Barbara, Janet, Pam, George, Jack – they all climbed up and grinned kindly at him. The kitten mewed.

'Here's your milk, you tiny little thing!' said Peter, and he poured some out of the bottle into the saucer he had brought. 'Janet, where's the bit of fish?'

The meeting was forgotten as the Seven crowded together on the little platform to watch the hungry kitten lap the milk and pounce on the fish. Jeff watched too. He smiled round gratefully at the children.

'Thanks,' he said. 'Thanks a lot!'

[10]

Jeff tries to remember

Peter had also brought a jar of peanut butter and a slab of cake for Jeff, and Colin had brought half a loaf and some butter. The boy took them hungrily, and didn't even wait to cut a slice of bread.

He tore at it with his teeth, and the others watched him, feeling shocked to see such hunger.

Janet gently took the bread from him, cut a large slice, buttered it and spread it thickly with peanut butter. 'You'll like this better than mouthfuls of bread!' she said.

Jeff ate everything they had brought, except the biscuits they were keeping for mid-morning. He wiped his mouth on the sleeve of his jacket with a sigh.

'That was good,' he said. 'I can't tell you how good!'

The kitten had finished its meal now too, and was sitting beside Jeff, washing its face.

'It looks fatter already,' said Janet, stroking it. 'Poor little thing! Imagine kicking a baby like this! You wouldn't think there'd be anyone bad enough, would you?'

'Mr Tizer's *very* bad,' said Jeff. 'Worse than my uncle. He kicks me too.'

'We want you to tell us all you can,' said Peter, settling himself as comfortably as he could, with his back to the tree-trunk. 'We think we ought to try and find out what it was that Mr Tizer and your uncle were so afraid you had overheard. They must have been planning something wrong – something that ought to be stopped.'

Jeff stared at them. 'Stopped? Who's going to stop it? Not me. Nor you either. Nobody can stop Mr Tizer, not even the police. Anyway I don't know anything.'

'Jeff, you must try and think,' said Colin. 'You said you were asleep in the sitting-room on the sofa when your uncle and Mr Tizer were planning something. You said you woke up and turned over, and they were angry with you because they thought you'd heard what they were talking about. You *must* be able to remember *something*!'

'I can't,' said Jeff, looking sullen.

Peter felt sure he could if he really wanted to. 'You're afraid of Mr Tizer,' he said. 'That's why you won't try to remember. It's mean of you. We've been sorry for you and the kitten and helped you. Now you should help us. We'll see you don't come to any harm.'

Jeff stroked the kitten, and it purred loudly. 'Well – you've been really kind,' he said at last. 'And I'll try to remember what I overheard. But it doesn't make any sense to me, and it won't to you, either!'

'Never mind. Tell us,' said Colin.

Jeff frowned as he tried to remember. 'Let me see,' he began. 'I was asleep – and I woke up – and I heard their voices . . .'

'Yes. Go on,' said Peter.

'I don't know what they were talking about,' said Jeff. 'I was too sleepy to hear properly. I just heard a few things – things that don't make any sense.'

'What things?' asked Barbara, wishing she could jog Jeff and make him go faster in his story.

'Well – let's see – they talked about MKX,' said Jeff, frowning hard. 'Yes, I remember that clearly, MKX.'

'MKX?' said Jack. 'What in the world does that mean? Would it be a code-word for someone helping them in their plans?'

'I don't know,' said Jeff. 'But I do remember MKX. And I remember a date too – Thursday the 25th. They said that two or three times. That's next Thursday, isn't it?'

'Yes,' said Peter. 'It is. Perhaps that was the date of their next robbery or whatever they were planning to do! I say, this is exciting. Go on, Jeff. Remember something else!'

'Don't hurry me,' said Jeff. 'Else I shall remember wrong.'

There was a dead silence at once. No one wanted Jeff to 'remember wrong'!

'They spoke about someone too,' said Jeff, wrinkling his forehead. 'Let's see. Yes – Emma Lane. They kept on about Emma Lane, I do remember that.'

'Emma Lane? That's a good clue,' said Colin. 'We might be able to find out who she is. I've never heard of her.'

'Anything else?' asked Peter. 'You really are doing very well, Jeff. Think hard.'

Jeff was pleased. He thought again, going back in his memory to that night on the sofa, hearing the two men's voices again in his mind.

'Oh, yes!' he said suddenly, 'they said something about a red pillow. That puzzled me. A red pillow. I remember that.'

It puzzled the others too. A red pillow didn't seem to fit into anything. Who would have a red pillow, and what for?

'MKX. Thursday the 25th. Emma Lane. A red pillow,' said Peter. 'What a mix-up! I can't make head or tail of any plot with those four things in it. In fact, the only thing that is at all possible to follow up is the Emma Lane clue. Anything more, Jeff? Think, do think!'

'There was something about a grating,' said Jeff. 'Watching through a grating – yes, that was it! Does that help you at all?'

No, it didn't. It just added to all the mystery! How were the Secret Seven to tackle all that?

[11]

Talking and planning

Jeff couldn't remember anything more at all. He began to look worried when the Seven pressed him. He went rather white, and Peter noticed it.

'All right. No more questions,' he said. 'We will discuss all this, and have a few biscuits to help us, and a drink of something. Like a biscuit, Jeff?'

Although it was only about an hour since he had eaten a huge meal, Jeff was quite ready to eat again. So was the kitten! It nibbled a biscuit that Janet held out to it, and was quite playful.

'It's feeling better,' said Jeff. 'Listen! Is that your dog barking?'

It was. Scamper barked a few little barks

at first, and then burst into loud and angry ones. Peter peered down the tree. Jeff clutched Colin, looking frightened.

'Don't give me away if it's me they're after!' he said. 'Please, please don't!'

Two men were below the tree, walking past. Peter made Jeff look down. He shrank back at once, looking so scared that Peter knew immediately that the men were Mr Tizer and Jeff's uncle. They were looking for him still, and were under the very tree that poor Jeff was in!

They didn't know that, of course. Scamper was taking all their attention. He capered round the men, pretending to snap and snarl. He didn't like them at all.

'Brute of a dog!' said one of the men, and picked up a dead branch. He flung it at Scamper. Peter went red with rage. It didn't hit Scamper, but it sent him quite mad! He flew at the two men, and they took to their heels at once!

Scamper chased them about a quarter of a mile through the woods, and then came back, panting, very pleased with himself.

'Good dog!' called down Peter, and Scamper wagged his tail at once. 'On guard again, Scamper, on guard!'

Scamper went to his tree and sat down. No dog could have looked more pleased or important. The Secret Seven sat back with a sigh of relief. Poor Jeff was white and trembling, and the kitten had gone into hiding under his torn coat.

'Cheer up, Jeff,' said Peter. 'Scamper has chased them away. I wonder how they guessed you were here.'

'I think it's because of the kitten,' said Jeff. 'They've only got to ask if anyone has seen a boy with a kitten. Several people in the wood have seen me about, foresters and walkers and such. Mr Tizer and my uncle will get me in the end.'

'No, they won't,' said Peter. 'I must say I

didn't like the look of them. Now – what are we going to do about this?'

The Seven talked and talked. MKX. Who or what was that? Emma Lane. How could they possibly find out where she lived? The red pillow. Impossible clue! The 25th. That was a definite date, but what was going to happen on it, and where? The grating. Where was that – and why was someone going to watch through it?

'I don't think even that famous detective Sherlock Holmes could have made head or tail of this,' said Peter, at last. 'It doesn't seem any use to discuss it at all.'

'No. But it's fun and very exciting,' said Pam. 'I think we ought to tell someone. What about your parents, Peter?'

'Yes. We'd better tell them,' said Peter, not wanting to in the least. 'If we could find out something ourselves, we would have a shot at it. But I don't see how we can. Except that we could find out if there *is*

an Emma Lane. That might lead us somewhere.'

'How could we?' asked Barbara.

'Ask at the post office,' said George,
feeling rather bright. 'They know where
everyone lives.'

'Yes. Good idea,' said Peter. 'You and Jack
can ask on the way home. And if it leads to
nothing we'll tell my father and mother.'

'I don't want you to,' said Jeff. 'I'll get
into trouble if the police go into this.'

'Sorry, Jeff,' said Peter. 'But this affair has
got to be sorted out. It's a pity it's beyond
the power of the Secret Seven. We've never
had a failure yet! Still – this really is too
difficult for anything!'

'We'd better go,' said George. 'I keep
getting into rows for being late. I bet you
others do too.'

'Yes, we do!' said Janet. 'And you and
Jack are going to call at the post office,
aren't you? We really must go.'

'When will you be back here again?' asked Jeff anxiously.

'This afternoon probably. Or after tea,' said Peter. 'We'll decide as we go home. We'll bring you some more food. Anyway, you can eat the rest of the biscuits and the chocolate. That will keep you going. Now don't look so scared. You'll be quite all right! No one can possibly guess you are up here.'

Jeff looked very doubtful. He watched the Seven climb down one by one. He heard Scamper's excited welcome. The kitten shrank back in fright against him when she heard the loud barks.

If Mr Tizer hears those barks, he'll guess something's up, thought poor Jeff in a panic. I may be safe up in this tree, but I've no way of escape if Mr Tizer found out I was here and climbed up after me!

[12]

Emma Lane

George and Jack called in at the post office as Peter had told them. They knew the post office girl, and she smiled at them.

'I hope it won't bother you to find out for us,' began George, very politely. 'But we want to know where someone called Emma Lane lives. It's rather important. Can you possibly tell us?'

'It will take me a few minutes,' said the girl taking down a big directory. 'I'll find out for you now.'

The boys waited patiently. The girl turned over page after page, running her finger down lists of names.

'Yes,' she said. 'There *is* an Emma Lane. Mrs Emma Lane, one, Church Street. That must be the one you want. It's the only Emma Lane there is. The others are Elizabeth and Elsie.'

'Oh *thanks*!' said George, delighted. 'One, Church Street. That's easy to remember!'

'We'll go and tell Peter after dinner,' said Jack. 'Then perhaps we could all go and find out exactly who Emma Lane is and what she does.'

So, after dinner, they went round to Peter's house and he and Janet listened with great interest to their bit of news.

'We'll go straightaway to Emma Lane's and see if we can find out anything at all,' said Peter. 'She might know Mr Tizer, for instance.'

'Yes. She might tell us something about him, and that awful uncle of Jeff's,' said George. 'Shall we get the others and all go together?'

'No,' said Peter. 'It might look a bit

peculiar, seven of us arriving to talk to Emma!'

They set off to Church Street. Number One was a dear little house, neat and pretty with a tiny well-kept front garden.

The four children stopped outside, and debated who was to go to the door and what to say.

'You go, Peter,' said George. 'We did our bit going to the post office. I wouldn't know *what* to say to Emma Lane!'

'All right. Janet and I will go,' said Peter, and he and his sister walked up the little path to the neat green front door. They rang the bell.

A small girl opened the door and stared at them. She didn't say a word.

'Er – could you tell me if Mrs Emma Lane is in?' asked Peter, politely.

'Who's she?' asked the little girl. 'I've never heard of any Emma Lane.'

This was most surprising. Peter was

puzzled. 'But the post office said she lived here,' he said. 'Isn't there an Emma Lane here? What about your mother?'

'My mother's called Mary Margaret Harris,' said the small girl. 'And I'm Lucy Ann Harris.'

A voice called up the hall passage. 'Who's that, Lucy?'

'I don't know,' called back Lucy. 'It's just two children asking for someone who doesn't live here.'

A lady came up the passage, her hands covered in flour. She smiled at Peter and Janet. 'I'm making cakes,' she said. 'Now, who is it you want?'

'They want an Emma Lane,' said the little girl, laughing. 'But she doesn't live here, does she, Mother?'

'Emma Lane? Why, she's your grandmother, you silly child!' said the lady. Lucy stared at her mother in surprise.

'I never knew Granny's name was

Emma,' she said. 'I never heard anyone call her Emma Lane. You call her Mother and I call her Granny.'

'Well, she's got a name, all the same,' said the lady. She turned to Peter and Janet. 'The old lady doesn't live here now,' she said. 'She went away three months ago to the seaside, and we've got her house instead. Did you want to speak to her?'

'No – well, yes – but it doesn't matter,' said Peter, feeling rather muddled. 'Thank you very much. I'm sorry to have bothered you in the middle of making cakes.'

He and Janet went down the path. 'What a silly girl not to know her grandmother's name,' said Janet.

'Well, do *you* know the names of our two grannies?' said Peter. 'We know their surnames, but I don't know the Christian name of either of our grannies! I've never heard anyone call them by name, except that *we* call them Granny, and our parents call them Mother.'

'Do you suppose that little girl's granny has anything to do with Mr Tizer's plans?' asked Janet. Peter shook his head.

'No, she's an old lady, and she must be nice if she lived in that lovely little house, and anyway she's not there. She's not the Emma Lane we want, and yet she was the only one the post office knew!'

They walked on in silence. Peter sighed. 'We had better tell Mummy and Daddy, Janet. It's all too muddled and difficult this time. There's not even anything we can do to unravel the muddle. A red pillow! MKX! It's just silly.'

[13]

A nasty shock

Daddy was in for tea. Peter broke the news to him while he was spreading slices of bread and butter with honey.

'Daddy! The Secret Seven are in the middle of something again!'

Daddy and Mummy both looked up at once. 'You and your Secret Seven! What's up this time?' said Daddy. 'Nothing serious, I hope.'

'We don't know,' said Peter. 'But as two of the people in it are supposed to be really bad – and I think they are – then it might be serious. But although we know quite a lot, it's all so silly and muddled and difficult that we can't make head or tail of it. So we thought we'd better tell *you*!'

'Fire ahead,' said Daddy. 'I can hardly wait to hear!'

'You're not to laugh, Daddy,' said Janet. 'The Secret Seven is a *proper* Society, and you know it's already done quite a lot of things.'

'I'm not really laughing,' said Daddy. 'Nor is Mummy. Tell us all about it.'

So Peter and Janet told the tale of their tree-house and Jeff and the kitten, and his wicked uncle and Mr Tizer, and all the curious collection of things that Jeff had remembered.

Daddy ate his tea all the time. He listened, asking a few questions now and again. Mummy listened too, exclaiming once or twice that she thought the tree-house sounded very dangerous. At last the tale came to an end.

'It certainly wants looking into,' said Daddy. 'But if you want my opinion, I think that boy Jeff has made most of it up. He's feeling miserable because his mother has gone into hospital, he doesn't like his uncle and aunt, he got into trouble with them, and ran away. And you were very kind to him, so he's made up a nice little tale!'

'Oh *no*, Daddy,' said Janet at once. 'He *didn't* make it up. He really didn't. And the kitten *was* hurt. Somebody *had* kicked it!'

'Well, look here, go and fetch that boy Jeff and bring him here to me,' said Daddy. 'If there's anything in his story I'll soon find out, and if there *is* any funny business going on we'll find that out too. He can tell us the address of his uncle, and the police can go and see if there's anything in his tale.'

'He doesn't want the police to be told,' said Peter.

'Of course he doesn't, if he's made up the tale!' said Daddy. 'Now you go and fetch him. Tell him I shan't bite his head off. As for all the things he says he remembers hearing when he was half-asleep, well, *I* think he dreamt them! Don't look so upset, both of you. When you get a bit older you'll learn not to believe all the tales people tell you!'

'But Daddy, he was speaking the truth, I'm sure he was,' said Janet, almost in tears.

'Right. Then we'll certainly do something to help him,' said Daddy. 'Go and get him now. I'll finish what I'm working on and be ready as soon as you get back.'

Peter and Janet set off rather gloomily to the tree-house. It was very, very damping to have Daddy and Mummy so certain that Jeff was a fraud. *They* didn't think he was. Well, now Jeff would have to go with them and tell Daddy everything. He would probably be so scared that he wouldn't say a word!

'I hope Jeff *will* come back with us,' said Peter, suddenly thinking that it might be very, very difficult to get him to climb down the tree if he didn't want to. They said no more till they got to the tree.

Peter called up. 'Jeff! Come on down! We've got something to tell you.'

Nobody answered. Peter called again. 'JEFF! It's me, Peter. Come on down. There's nobody here but me and Janet. It's important.'

There was no reply. But wait – yes, there was! A tiny little mew sounded from up above. The kitten!

'The kitten's there,' said Peter. 'So Jeff must be there too. I wonder if he's all right? I'll go up and see.'

Up he went. He climbed up on to the platform which was still strewn with cushions. The kitten ran to him, mewing.

There wasn't a sign of Jeff! Peter called again and peered upwards, thinking the boy might have climbed higher. No – he wasn't there either! Then he caught sight of a piece of paper stuck into a crevice of the tree-trunk. Peter took it and read it.

'They've found me,' said the note. 'They

say they'll come up and throw the kitten down the tree if I don't climb down to them. They would too. Take care of the kitten – and thanks for everything. Jeff.'

Peter slithered down the tree so quickly that he grazed his hands and knees. He held out the paper to Janet. 'Look at that! They've found him. They must have come back again, guessing he might be up here, with Scamper barking round like that. Poor Jeff!'

Janet looked upset and alarmed. 'Oh dear – *now* what are we to do? We don't even know where Jeff lives. We can't find out anything, or help him. Oh look, that poor little kitten is coming down the tree all by itself!'

Peter lifted it down. It mewed. 'We'll look after you all right,' he said. 'Where has your master gone to? That's what *we'd* like to know!'

[14]

George gets an idea

Peter and Janet went home, the kitten cuddled against Peter. Daddy was waiting for them.

'Well – where's the boy Jeff?' he said.

'He's gone,' said Peter, and showed his father the note.

'You won't hear of *him* again,' said Daddy. 'I tell you, it was just a made-up tale. Forget it! Ask your mother if you can keep the kitten, though we don't really want another cat. I don't think much of the boy, deserting the kitten like that!'

'He didn't, Daddy,' said Janet, trying not to cry. 'He *had* to leave it. Those men were cruel.'

Daddy went back to his work. Peter and

Janet looked at one another. Daddy was so often right about things. Perhaps he was right about this too. Perhaps Jeff *had* been a fraud, and made up a tale to tell them.

'What are we going to do?' asked Janet, wiping her eyes. Peter considered.

'We'll have to give it up,' he said. 'We can't very well go against what Daddy says, and we *know* we can't do anything ourselves, because we don't understand what any of the things Jeff remembered can possibly mean. And now Jeff is gone, and we don't know where, we can't even get him to tell his tale to anyone!'

'We'll have to call a meeting and tell the others,' said Janet, gloomily. 'They won't like it. It sounded so exciting at first, now it's just a silly make-up. And I liked Jeff, too.'

'So did I,' said Peter. 'Let's write notes and slip them into the letterboxes to tell the others there will be a meeting tomorrow. Down in the shed, I think, for a change.'

The notes were written and delivered. At ten o'clock the next morning the Seven collected together in the shed. The password 'Adventure' seemed most disappointing to Janet and Peter now that there *was* no adventure.

'I've got gloomy news,' said Peter. 'We told Daddy everything, and he didn't believe it. He told us to fetch Jeff, and promised to listen to his story – but Jeff was gone!'

Everyone was startled. 'Gone!' said Jack. 'Where?'

Peter produced the note and everyone read it solemnly. 'We've got the kitten,' said Peter. 'And that's all that's left of Jeff and his peculiar tale.'

'So we can't go on with anything,' said George, in dismay. 'I was just getting all worked up about it, thinking we were in for another excitement.'

'I know. But we were wrong,' said Peter.

'This affair is closed. We can't go any further or find out anything more. It's our first failure.'

It was a very gloomy meeting indeed. Everyone felt very flat. They wondered where Jeff was. Had he *really* cheated them and told them a made-up tale? It was very difficult to believe.

'We saw Mr Tizer and Jeff's uncle, you know,' said Colin, suddenly. '*They* couldn't have been made up.'

'We've only got Jeff's word for it that they were his uncle and Mr Tizer,' Peter reminded him. 'He certainly said they were, but for all we know they might have been two foresters, or even poachers. They looked pretty nasty, anyway.'

There was a silence. 'All right,' said George at last. 'It's finished. We don't do anything more. Are we going to the tree-house today?'

'I don't feel like it somehow, this morning,' said Janet. 'Does anyone? I feel disappointed and rather cross.'

Everyone laughed. Janet was hardly ever cross. Colin patted her on the back. 'Cheer up! We'll soon get over it. And anyway, finished or not, I'm still going to keep my eyes open! Who knows – I might meet Emma Lane walking down the street, carrying a red pillow embroidered with the letters MKX!'

That made everyone roar with laughter. They said goodbye and went off feeling more cheerful. 'What's the date?' said George to Colin, as they went down the lane together. 'Wednesday the 24th, isn't it? Well, it's tomorrow that things were supposed to happen, according to Jeff.'

'He probably made up the date,' said Colin. 'What are we going to do this morning? We've plenty of time left.'

'Let's go down to the canal,' said George.

'We may see some barges going along. I like the canal, it's so long and straight and quiet.'

'I like it too,' said Colin. 'I'll go and get my boat. You get yours too. Meet me in that road that goes under the railway bridge, down by the canal.'

'What road?' asked George, but Colin had already gone. George raised his voice. 'Colin! What road do you mean? I don't want to miss you!'

'You know the road, idiot,' yelled back Colin. 'It's EMBER LANE!'

Colin was so far away by this time that it was difficult to catch what he said. It sounded like 'EMMA LANE'. George stood rooted to the spot. Ember Lane. *Emma Lane.* Jeff might have mis-heard what his uncle had said – it was probably Ember Lane he meant, not Emma Lane! They sounded so much the same. EMBER LANE!

'It might be that. It might be,' said George to himself in excitement. 'We'll have a really good look round Ember Lane – just *in case*!'

[15]

The red pillow

With their boats the two boys met at the beginning of Ember Lane. George began to tell Colin excitedly what he thought.

'When you called out Ember Lane it sounded exactly like *Emma* Lane,' he said. 'Suppose that's what Jeff meant? He might have heard wrong, he was half-asleep. Ember Lane. I'm sure that was what it was.'

'And you think something was to happen in Ember Lane on the 25th?' said Colin, looking very thrilled. 'Gosh, you may be right. But what could happen here?'

They looked round Ember Lane. Although it was called a lane, it was nothing of the sort, though it might have been years ago.

It was a rather wide, dirty street, with great warehouses on either side. It led down to the canal. There were a good many people about, taking parcels from the warehouses, and running messages. It was difficult to imagine any robbery or anything out of the way taking place here.

Colin and George examined the street very carefully. They came to one warehouse that had a grating let into the bottom of the wall. They peered down. People were in an underground room below, busy packing up parcels. The grating gave them a little light and air, though it also let in the dust.

'Well, there's a *grating*!' said George, standing up after peering through for some time. 'I suppose someone could stand here and watch through it, as Jeff said, but what would be the point?'

'Someone might watch from the *other* side of the grating,' said Colin. 'If he stood on that table down there, look, he could peer into the street through the grating. If the place was in darkness, he wouldn't be seen peering out. It would be quite a good place to watch from.'

'It might,' said George. 'Yes, it might. A grating to watch through in Ember Lane. This is rather good! Are we on the track of anything, do you think?'

'Probably not!' said Colin. 'If we are we shall probably spot a red pillow on a sofa somewhere, or hear someone hissing, "MKX, you're wanted"!'

They went to sail their boats on the canal till dinner-time. Then they went home, peeping through the grating at the foot of the warehouse in Ember Lane as they went. The underground room below was empty now. The workers had gone to lunch.

'We'd better tell Peter,' said Colin as they parted. 'Let's go along this afternoon and tell him. He ought to know, I think, even though there may be nothing in it.'

Peter was most interested. 'That's bright of you,' he said. 'Emma Lane. Ember Lane. Anyone could mishear that quite easily. But I don't think so much of the grating. There are gratings everywhere.'

'Not in Ember Lane,' said Colin. 'We looked, and that's the only one.'

'Janet and I will go along and have a look at Ember Lane this afternoon,' said Peter. 'And the grating.'

They went. Ember Lane looked gloomy and dirty. Janet and Peter examined the grating with interest. Colin was right. There *was* only one in Ember Lane.

'Well, it doesn't tell us much,' said Peter. 'Even if we decided that this was the grating through which Mr Tizer or someone was going to watch, *why* should they want to watch? And what? It's no crime to peer through a grating.'

'They might want to watch unseen for something or someone, so that they could signal his coming to somebody waiting to pounce,' said Janet. Peter stared at her, most impressed.

'Yes. That's exactly what they *might* do!' he said. 'But what could they see from there? Let's stand with our backs to the grating and see if we can spot what would be within their sight.'

They stood and looked hard, their eyes ranging over the warehouse opposite, the pavement, and a lamp-post.

'Well, all that could be seen from behind that grating is the warehouse opposite, though not all of it,' said Janet. 'And the lamp-post, and the pavement near it, and that red pillar-box. Yes, I'm sure that red pillar-box could be seen too.'

Janet suddenly stopped. She caught her breath and looked round at Peter, her eyes shining. 'Peter,' she said, 'Peter! The red pillow!'

'The red pillow? Where?' said Peter,

puzzled. 'Oh, Janet – JANET! I see what you mean! It wasn't a red *pillow* that Jeff heard, it was red *pillar-box*. And there it is!'

The two stared at the red pillar-box, thinking hard. A girl went up to it and posted some letters. Peter and Janet felt absolutely certain that 'red pillow' meant 'red pillar-box'. And it could be watched from behind the only grating in Ember Lane.

'We're getting somewhere,' said Peter, suddenly feeling quite out of breath. 'Jeff *did* hear something. His tale wasn't made up – but because he was half-asleep when he heard the men talking, he didn't hear properly.'

'If only we could find what MKX was,' said Janet. 'But we can't. I expect all the men in Mr Tizer's gang have numbers or letters. But we're certainly putting a few of the jigsaw pieces together, Peter. Let's go and tell the others!'

[16]

And now MKX

Every member of the Secret Seven felt excited when they heard the latest news. They thought that Janet had been very clever in realising that the red pillow was a mistake for red pillar-box.

Barbara thought for a moment and then said that she wondered if the man watching behind the grating might be waiting to signal to someone when the postman came to empty the box.

'Someone might be waiting to steal the letters from him,' she said.

'That's an idea,' said Peter. 'But there isn't much point in stealing ordinary letters. They're not worth anything!'

'That's true,' said Jack. 'It's sacks of

registered parcels and letters that are usually stolen. They're worth something. But not
ordinary letters. I don't somehow think the
watcher is watching the pillar-box, he's
probably watching for someone waiting
there, or passing it.'

'Is it worth telling Daddy all this, Janet,
do you suppose?' said Peter, after the Seven
had discussed everything thoroughly. 'After
all – it's tomorrow *something* has been
planned to happen. We haven't much time
left.'

'Well – we might tell him this evening,'
said Janet. 'Let's wait till then. We might
think of something else important. I don't
think Daddy will change his mind about
things just because we've discovered that a
red pillar-box can be watched through a
grating in Ember Lane.'

'It does sound rather silly put like that,'
said Peter. 'Well – we'll wait till this evening. Goodbye till then.'

But before they could tell their father of their latest ideas, Pam came dashing into the garden to find Peter and Janet. Barbara was just behind.

They found Peter and Janet watering their gardens. Pam flung herself on them.

'Peter! Janet! What do you think? We've seen MKX!'

Janet dropped her watering-can, startled. Peter stared in excitement.

'Who is he? Where did you see him?'

'It isn't a he. It's a van!' said Barbara. 'Pam and I were going home together, when we saw a post-office van standing near a pillar-box – you know, a mail-van, painted red.'

'And its letters were MKX!' cried Pam. 'MKX 102. What do you think of that? We couldn't believe our eyes when we saw it was MKX. I'm sure that's what Jeff meant – the mail-van, MKX.'

'But – but there must be plenty of cars with the letters MKX,' said Peter. 'Plenty.'

'Not in one place,' said Pam. 'I don't ever remember seeing MKX in our town before. I notice car numbers, because I want to see if I can spot a Z something someday. I haven't yet. Peter! That van *must* be the MKX those men spoke about when Jeff was half-asleep.'

Peter sat down on a garden-seat. 'I think you're right,' he said. 'Yes – I think you must be right. It's all beginning to fit in. Wait now, let's work it out.'

He sat up and thought, frowning hard. 'Yes, perhaps a mail van goes into Ember Lane, with a few sacks of registered parcels inside. The postman gets out of his van to go across to the red pillar-box to collect the letters.'

'Yes! YES!' cried Pam. 'And someone is watching through the grating to see when he is unlocking the pillar-box, with his back to the van, and signals to the others who are waiting out of sight somewhere . . .'

'And at once they see the signal, rush to the van, and drive it off before the postman can get back to it!' cried Janet, taking the words out of Pam's mouth.

They all sat and looked at one another, their eyes shining. They felt breathless. Had they solved everything, or was it just too clever to be true?

'Well, I shall certainly tell Daddy now,' said Peter, thrilled. 'What a bit of luck you noticed the letters on that mail-van, Pam and Barbara. Good work! We're a really great Secret Society, I think. Successes every time!'

'And we thought this one was a failure!' said Janet. 'Look, there's Daddy. Come and tell him now.'

So Peter's father was soon surrounded by four excited children, determined to make him believe that what they had discovered REALLY MATTERED!

He listened carefully. He pursed up his

mouth and gave his head a little scratch, looking with twinkling eyes at the children. 'Well, well, this is rather a different tale this time. Most ingenious! Yes, I'll do something about it.'

He went inside and rang up the Inspector of Police, and asked him to come along. 'I've a curious tale to tell you,' he said. 'You may or may not believe it, but I think you ought to hear it.'

And before ten minutes had passed the kind-faced Inspector was sitting in the garden, listening solemnly to the children's tale.

He glanced at Peter's father when they had finished. 'This is important,' he said. 'There have been too many mail-van robberies lately. We'll catch the ringleaders this time, thanks to the valiant Secret Seven!'

[17]

Top Secret

He got up to go. The children pressed round him. 'Tell us what you are going to do! Do, do tell us!'

'I'm going to discuss the whole matter with other people,' said the Inspector, smiling down at the four children. 'You've not given me much time to make preparations, you know! According to you, it's all fixed for tomorrow!'

'How shall we know what's going to happen?' asked Pam. 'It's *our* affair this – can't we see what's going to happen?'

'I'll let you know tomorrow, at ten o'clock,' said the big Inspector, twinkling at them. 'Call a meeting of your Secret Society down in the shed, and I'll be there to report to you!'

There was such excitement that evening among the Secret Seven that their parents thought they would never get them to bed. Colin, George and Jack were all told by the other four, and spent a wonderful time thinking how clever they had been.

'Well, we'll meet down in the shed at ten tomorrow,' said Colin. 'Passwords, and everything, and you all realise, of course, that not one single word of what the Inspector tells us is to be told to ANYONE ELSE.'

'Of course,' said everyone.

At five to ten they had all arrived at the shed except the Inspector. He came promptly at ten o'clock.

'Have to let him in without the password,' said Peter. But Janet called out loudly. 'Password, please!'

The Inspector grinned to himself outside the shed. 'Well,' he said, 'I don't know it, but there's one word that seems to me to be a very good password for you at the moment, and that is – ADVENTURE!'

'Right!' shouted everyone in delight, and the door opened. In went the Inspector and was given a large box to sit on. He beamed round at them all.

'This is SECRET,' he said. 'Top secret. We've made inquiries, and we think it is possible that a robbery may be planned this evening when the postman drives up in his mail-van to make the seven-thirty collection of letters from the red pillar-box in Ember Lane. At that time of the evening he has on board his van some sacks of registered letters.'

'Oooooh!' said Pam. 'Just what we thought!'

'Now what we are going to do is this,' said the Inspector. 'A postman will drive up as usual with the mail-van. He will park it in the usual place. He will go across to the pillar-box and unlock it, with his back to the van.'

'Yes,' said everyone, hanging on to the Inspector's words. 'What next?'

'Well, the watcher behind the grating will probably signal to others waiting opposite in hiding,' said the Inspector. 'They will rush to the van, jump into the driver's seat, two of them probably, and drive it away.'

'But, will you let them do that?' said Pam. 'With all the sacks inside!'

'The sacks won't be inside, my dear,' said the Inspector. 'But six fine policemen will, and WHAT a shock for the two men when they park the mail-van somewhere lonely and go to unlock the van door.'

'Oh!' cried the Seven, and gazed at the Inspector in delight.

'And the man signalling behind the grating will find two policemen waiting for him in the passage outside the underground room,' said the big Inspector. 'Very interesting; don't you think so?'

'Please – PLEASE can we be somewhere and watch?' asked Peter. 'After all, if it hadn't been for us you wouldn't have known anything about this.'

'Well now, you listen,' said the Inspector, dropping his voice low and making everything sound twice as exciting. 'There's a warehouse called Mark Donnal's in Ember Lane, and it's got a back entrance in the road behind, Petton Road. Nobody will say anything if seven children go in one by one, and make their way to a window overlooking Ember Lane at the front of the warehouse. In fact, I wouldn't be surprised if there isn't someone there to show you the very room you want!'

Every single one of the Secret Seven wanted to hug the big Inspector, but as he got up at that moment, they couldn't. They beamed in delight at him.

'Thank you! It's marvellous of you! We'll be there, if our parents let us.'

'I think you'll find that will be all right,' said the Inspector, and off he went.

'WELL!' said Peter, looking round. 'This is wonderful. Seats in the very front row.'

'Yes. But we shan't be able to see the best bit of all, when the men open the van, and out come the policemen!' said Jack.

'Never mind, we'll see plenty!' said Peter. 'I wonder where Jeff is. I suppose that awful Mr Tizer took him away and locked him up somewhere till the raid was over. I wonder what will happen to poor old Jeff.'

'Mew,' said the kitten, who was on Janet's knee. Its leg was healed now, and it was a fat, amusing little thing. Janet hugged it.

'I expect poor Jeff misses you,' she said. 'Never mind, maybe we'll be able to do something for Jeff if he's found, and you can go back to him.'

'I wish tonight was here,' said George, getting up. 'It'll never come!'

But it did come, and it brought a most exciting evening with it!

[18]

An exciting finish

The Seven spent the rest of the morning up in the tree-house, talking over everything. Scamper put himself on guard as usual, but no one came by. The afternoon dragged on, and tea-time came. Then the children began to feel intensely excited.

At half-past six they went one by one down to Ember Lane. They thought they had better not go in a bunch in case they attracted attention. They found the back entrance of Mark Donnal's warehouse in Petton Road, and went up the steps to it. The door swung open silently as they reached the top step. Most mysterious!

But behind it, keeping guard, was one of the village policemen! He grinned at each child as he or she walked in, and took them up the stairs, along dusty passages, to a little room at the front.

'We've got a marvellous view of the red pillar-box,' said Janet to Peter. 'We shall see everything. I wonder if the signaller is down behind the grating yet.'

They asked the policeman. He nodded. 'Yes, he's there all right. We've watched him go into the underground room, complete with white handkerchief for signalling. There are now two policemen in a cupboard outside the door, waiting!'

It was too exciting to be borne! The children simply couldn't sit still. The time went by slowly. Seven o'clock – ten-past – twenty-past – twenty-five-past . . .

A clock on a nearby church tower suddenly chimed the half hour. Half-past seven! Now was the time!

Everything happened very suddenly and quickly. There came the roar of a car-engine, and round a corner came the red mail-van, MKX 102. It stopped and the driver jumped out. He took a sack and ran across to the red pillar-box. He unlocked it, his back to his van.

And then two men suddenly came from a small alley-way and sprinted at top speed to the van. There was no one in Ember Lane except the postman. All the workers had gone home long ago.

But many watchers saw the two men. The seven children stared breathlessly, so did the policeman with them, so did the signaller behind the grating.

And so did many hidden eyes belonging to watchful police, including the Inspector himself!

The men leapt into the front of the van. One got into the driving-seat, the other next to him. There was a roar of the engine, and the van drove off at top speed, vanishing round the corner.

The postman straightened up. He didn't seem surprised. He was in the secret too! The children rocked to and fro on their seats in excitement. A few policemen appeared from odd places and spoke to one another. Then there came a noise from down below!

'That's the signaller being caught!' said Peter. 'I bet it is!'

It was, of course. He had walked out of the underground room straight into the arms of the waiting policemen. And, lo and behold, it was Mr Tizer!

But the evening's excitement wasn't yet finished! Before half an hour had gone, the mail-van was back again, but this time it was driven by a uniformed policeman, with another beside him. Inside were the two men. As the children watched, the van doors were opened, and four policemen got out with the two men held firmly by the arms.

'Got them nicely,' said the policeman who was in the room with the children. 'They must have parked quite nearby, opened the van, and got the surprise of their lives, and here they are, back again to talk to the Chief!'

It was maddening to have to go home after that. What an excitement! How wonderful to be in at the finish, but how dull afterwards!

The Seven went to Peter's house to supper, talking all at once. Nobody could possibly hear what anyone else said. And waiting at the house for them was – Jeff! The kitten was back in his arms, and he looked scared but happy.

'Hallo,' he said. 'The police know all about everything now, don't they? They came to my uncle's house and found me. Uncle had locked me up in an attic. I haven't got to go back to him any more.'

'What's going to happen to you then?' asked Peter.

'They're trying to find out about my mother,' said Jeff, hugging the kitten. 'I told you I didn't even know what hospital she'd gone to. I'm to stay here till they know. Your mother said I could.'

Jeff looked clean and his hair was brushed. Peter's mother had felt sorry for him and had done what she could when the police brought him to her. Now he was to have supper with the Seven. He was very happy.

The telephone rang, and Peter's mother went to answer it. She came back, smiling. 'It's about your mother, Jeff,' she said. 'She's better! She's leaving hospital tomorrow and going back home, and you're to be there to greet her!'

Jeff stood with tears in his eyes. He couldn't say a word. He held the kitten so tightly that it mewed. He turned to the Seven, finding his tongue at last.

'It's you that have done all this!' he said,

stammering in his joy. 'It's all because of you. I'm glad I found your tree-house. I'm glad I met you. You're a wonderful Secret Society, the best in all the world!'

'Well, we do feel rather pleased with ourselves tonight,' said Peter, grinning at Jeff. 'Don't we, Scamper, old boy? Do *you* agree that we're a good Secret Society? Do you agree that we must go on and do lots more exciting things?'

'Woof,' said Scamper and thumped his tail on the floor. 'woof!'

Well done, Secret Seven! Do let's hear your next adventure soon.

h HODDER

A complete list of the SECRET SEVEN
ADVENTURES *by Enid Blyton*

A complete list of the FAMOUS FIVE
ADVENTURES *by Enid Blyton*